The Story of the Little Mole who went in Search of Whodunit

The Story of the Little Mole who went in Search of Whodunit

by Werner Holzwarth & Wolf Erlbruch

Abrams Image
New York

When Little Mole poked his head out of his mole hole one day to see if the sun was shining, Something very strange happened.

(It was long and brown and looked a little bit like a hot dog. Worst of all, it landed right on top of Little Mole's head.)

Little Mole asked a pigeon who was just flying by, "Did you do this on my head?"

Then Little Mole asked a horse who was grazing in the field, "Did you do this on my head?"

Then Little Mole asked a hare who was happily munching a carrot, "Did you do this on my head?"

Then Little Mole asked a goat who was daydreaming, "Did you do this on my head?"

Then Little Mole asked a cow who was chewing her cud, "Did you do this on my head?"

Me? Certainly not me," said the cow. "I do mine like this."

(Swush-dup-dup—a big flat cow pie sploshed onto the ground. Little Mole was glad that it wasn't the cow whodunit on his head!)

Then Little Mole asked a fat, pink pig, "Did you do this on my head?"

"Me? Not me," answered the pig, "I do mine like this."

Splidgedy - splodge — a soft brown, smelly heap landed at his feet. Pee-ew! Little Mole had to hold his nose.

Little Mole looked around for another suspect, but all he saw were two fat flies. Dining! "At long last," Little Mole thought, "I bet they can help me." "Can you tell me who did this on my head?" asked Little Mole.

"Keep still a second," buzzed the two flies, busily studying what was on top of Little Mole's head.

A moment later they shouted triumphantly, "No question about it. It was a DOG!"

A dog? Of course! Now Little Mole wa: sure whodunit on his head.

As quick as a flash Little Mole climbed on top of Henry's doghouse.

(Pling!—a little brown crescent landed slap-dab in the middle of Henry's forehead.)

The deed done, a happy and satisfied Little Mole disappeared back into his mole hole.

Library of Congress Cataloging-in-Publication Data:

Holzwarth, Werner.

[Vom kleinen Maulwurf, der wissen wolte, we ihm auf den Kopf gemacht hat. English]

The Story of the Little Mole who went in search of whodunit/by Werner Holzwarth & Wolf Erlbruch

p. cm.

Summary: When Little Mole tries to find out who pooped on his head, the other animals show him how they poop in order to prove their innocence.

ISBN 13: 978-0-8109-4457-2

ISBN 10: 0-8109-4457-X

[1. Defecation–Fiction 2. Moles (Animals) – Fiction 3. Animals– Fiction 4. Humorous stories] I. Erlbruch, Wolf. II. Title

PZ7.H74365St   1993

[E]–dc20   93–17676

CIP

Copyright © 1989/2007 Peter Hammer Verlag

Hand lettering by Wendy Wilson

Originally published in 1989 by Peter Hammer Verlag

Published in 2007 by Abrams Image,

An imprint of ABRAMS

Printed and bound in China

10 9 8 7 6 5 4

THE ART OF BOOKS SINCE 1949

115 West 18th Street

New York, NY 10011

www.abramsbooks.com